## THIS WALKER BOOK BELONGS TO:

A nella page webb

*For Benedict*
E.B.

*For my sisters*
E.H.

First published 1975 by Ernest Benn Ltd
This edition published 1992 by
Walker Books Ltd, 87 Vauxhall Walk
London SE11 5HJ

Text © 1975 Elisabeth Beresford
Illustrations © 1992 Edgar Hodges
Illustrations based on original film puppets
designed by Ivor Wood © 1972 FilmFair

Printed and bound in Hong Kong by Imago

British Library Cataloguing in Publication Data
A catalogue record for this book is available
from the British Library.
ISBN 0-7445-1770-2
ISBN 0-7445-2154-8 (Pbk)

# WELLINGTON AND THE BLUE BALLOON

Written by

ELISABETH BERESFORD

Illustrations by EDGAR HODGES

*based on the original film puppets*

*designed by Ivor Wood*

WALKER BOOKS
LONDON

It had been very windy in the night so that when Great Uncle Bulgaria, Bungo and Wellington Womble came out of their burrow they saw that there was rubbish *everywhere*. The wind had blown newspapers and bags and packets and bits of *this* and pieces of *that* everywhere. What a mess the Common was in.

"Off you go, young Wombles," said Great Uncle Bulgaria, "and tidy up all this rubbish as fast as you can." Bungo and Wellington each had their tidy-bags firmly in their paws.

Just at that moment, an extra large gust of wind blew all the leaves and bits and pieces into the air. "Dear me," said Great Uncle Bulgaria. "What a lot of work there is to be sure. The first Womble to fill a tidy-bag and bring it back to the burrow shall have two helpings of dinner!"

"I'm sure I shall get back to the burrow first because I work faster than you do," said Bungo to Wellington. Bungo is a very bossy Womble. He always thinks he knows best about everything.

"Yes, I expect you will," said Wellington. Wellington is the smallest and shyest of the Wombles.

Bungo tidied up all kinds of things. Bags
and newspapers and packets and pieces of
this and that, and he put them all into his
tidy-bag. Wellington was working hard too,

but he wasn't as quick as Bungo. It took him
more time to put the rubbish into his tidy-
bag. He couldn't quite work out why he was
finding it so difficult.

"Oh dear!" said Wellington. The wind was still blowing, and the rubbish kept blowing about too.

It seemed to have a mind of its own. It wasn't easy to pick it up ... or even to get hold of it ...

except when the wind changed. It was all very awkward.

Bungo had tidied up all kinds of rubbish. His tidy-bag was nearly full and he was sure that he would be the Womble who would have two helpings of dinner. "I am sure that I have got a lot more than Wellington already," he said to himself.

He looked round to see what Wellington had done. Wellington was in trouble. He had got his scarf caught in a bush. While he was trying to get free, he noticed a small bit of blue rubbish. Bungo saw it too. "You can take that if you like," he said. "It's not very big." Wellington picked it up and looked at it. It was a balloon. "It's a blue balloon," said Wellington. "I wonder if I can blow it up?" He took a deep breath and began to blow.

The more Wellington blew, the bigger the balloon became. It got bigger and BIGGER and BIGGER. It grew even bigger than Wellington himself.

"What a jolly fine balloon," said Wellington admiringly. "It's – Whoops !" Just then there was a very strong gust of wind. Before Wellington knew what was happening, he was being blown along...

Harder and harder blew the wind and faster and FASTER and FASTER went Wellington.

He ran across the grass
and down a slope and up a small
hill. He had no breath left. And just as
he got to the top of the small hill there was
a very strong gust of wind…

The next thing Wellington knew was that
his feet weren't on the ground anymore. He
looked down and the ground had vanished!
"Help!" shouted Wellington, clinging on to
the blue balloon for all he was worth.
"Put me down. Stop it! I'm flying."
But there was no one to help him.

Bungo heard a shout, but he couldn't understand where it was coming from. There was no Womble to the left of him or to the right of him. "Must have imagined it," he said. And he went on tidying up.

"Help," shouted Wellington again, as he was blown higher and HIGHER and HIGHER. He hung on to the blue balloon and shut his eyes tightly. It was a very strange feeling being blown up into the sky. It was a bit like going up in a fast lift except that it didn't feel very safe.

Up and up and up went Wellington and the blue balloon. He was so high up now that he could see all over the Common. He could see Bungo with his tidy-bag almost overflowing. He was standing by the windmill looking very busy and important.

And Wellington could see Tomsk swimming in the lake. He was looking for water rubbish because he could swim best of all the Wombles.

Tomsk paused to take a breath. "Funny sort of bird that," he said. "Sort of blue. I must ask Great Uncle Bulgaria about it…"

And Wellington could see Orinoco fast asleep beside a bramble bush. Orinoco should have been tidying up rubbish like all the other Wombles, but instead he was having a nice forty winks and dreaming about dinner time. Lazy Orinoco.

And last of all, Wellington could see Great Uncle Bulgaria standing in front of the burrow. He was looking out across the Common and trying to see which of the young Wombles had tidied up the most rubbish.

All that Great Uncle Bulgaria, Bungo, Tomsk and Orinoco could hear was the noise of the wind. None of them had noticed that up in the sky was a big blue balloon and a very small Womble.

Then all of a sudden, something even more frightening happened to Wellington. There was a small "plop-plop-plop" sound. Suddenly, with a nasty hissing noise the big blue balloon began to get smaller and smaller and smaller. The big blue balloon had a hole in it!

Down, down, down, fell Wellington – the Common got closer and closer. "Help!" he shouted once more and then he shut his eyes…

And down came Wellington as light as a
leaf and right in front of the burrow. He
didn't hurt himself at all, because a big
plastic bag he had tidied up had made a

parachute for him. So when he opened his
eyes he was safe and sound and very close to
home! And he still had his tidy-bag, full of
rubbish, held firmly in one paw.

Great Uncle Bulgaria *was* surprised.

"Well done, young Wellington," said Great Uncle Bulgaria. "You are the first Womble to get back home and *what* a lot of rubbish you have tidied up to be sure. You shall have two helpings of dinner all right. How did you manage to get back to the burrow so quickly?"

"I'm not sure about that," said Wellington, shyly. "But I *am* sure that I am very, VERY, VERY hungry. What's for dinner?"

# MORE WALKER PAPERBACKS
## For You to Enjoy

### THE WOMBLES OF WIMBLEDON
by Elisabeth Beresford / Edgar Hodges

### ORINOCO RUNS AWAY
Orinoco gets into trouble when he dips his paws into
Madame Cholet's cake mixture!
ISBN 0-7445-2127-0   £2.99

### THE SNOW WOMBLE
One morning, the Wombles wake up to find their common covered in snow.
Orinoco thinks it's ice-cream and tries to eat it. Tomsk takes a
tray and goes tobogganing.
Bungo, meanwhile, builds a very familiar-looking snow Womble!
ISBN 0-7445-2128-9   £2.99

### THE MacWOMBLE'S PIPE BAND
When Cairngorm The MacWomble comes down from Scotland to visit,
he finds the rain has driven all the humans away from the common, which
means there is no rubbish for the Wombles to collect. No one remains
idle for long, though, when the MacWomble is calling the tune!
ISBN 0-7445-2152-1   £2.99

**Walker Paperbacks are available from most booksellers, or by post from
Walker Books Ltd, PO Box 11, Falmouth, Cornwall TR10 9EN.**

To order, send: title, author, ISBN number and price for each book ordered, your full name and address
and a cheque or postal order for the total amount, plus postage and packing:

UK and BFPO Customers – £1.00 for first book, plus 50p for the second book and plus 30p for each additional book to a maximum charge of £3.00.
Overseas and Eire Customers – £2.00 for first book, plus £1.00 for the second book and plus 50p per copy for each additional book.
Prices are correct at time of going to press, but are subject to change without notice.